Enid Blyton™

TOY TOWN STORIES

TUBBY BEAR'S TEA PARTY

First published in Great Britain by HarperCollins Publishers Ltd in 1997

1 3 5 7 9 10 8 6 4 2

Copyright © 1997 Enid Blyton Company Ltd. Enid Blyton's
signature mark is a Registered Trade Mark of Enid Blyton Ltd.

ISBN: 0 00 172012 0

Story by Fiona Cummings
Cover design and illustrations by County Studios
A CIP catalogue for this title is available from the British Library.
Printed and bound in Singapore

Enid Blyton™

TOY TOWN STORIES

TUBBY BEAR'S TEA PARTY

Collins

An Imprint of HarperCollinsPublishers

It was a fine, warm morning in Toyland.

"Just the kind of day for a tea party," said Mrs Tubby Bear. "Run along Master Tubby and see if you can stop Noddy as he drives past. Then we can invite him in for tea."

Tubby Bear was always full of mischief, and today was no different. He rushed out into the garden and could hear the Parp! Parp! of Noddy's car coming along the road.

For fun, Tubby did a few cartwheels across the lawn. Then he stood on his hands on the garden wall, and pulled a very nasty face as Noddy went by.

Just to make sure that
the little car stopped,
Tubby threw his
ball at Noddy's hat.
The bell

JINGLED loudly.

"You naughty bear!" said Noddy crossly. "You
did that on purpose! You could
have hurt me."

He threw the ball back to Tubby. The bear just laughed.

"I am sorry, Noddy," said Mrs Tubby Bear, appearing at the door. "Master Tubby is in high spirits because we're going to have a tea party. Would you and Big-Ears like to come?"

"Ooh, yes please!" said Noddy excitedly. "I'll go and tell Big-Ears now. What time shall we come?"

"At four o'clock," replied Mrs Tubby Bear.

"Can I come in your car to tell Big-Ears?" asked Master Tubby.

"No, you may not!" said Noddy crossly. "You are too naughty and I might have an accident." And off he drove.

"Never mind," Mrs Tubby told her son gently. "You can help me make the cakes for tea."

They went into the kitchen and got all the ingredients ready.

"Right, we need flour and eggs and milk and sugar," said Mrs Tubby Bear. She put everything on to the table and got out her *best* mixing bowl.

"Now Tubby," she said. "You mustn't touch anything until I tell you to. We don't want everything getting in a muddle, do we?"

"No," said Tubby, looking mischievously at the table.

"Wait until I've put on my apron," said Mrs Tubby, "then we can start our baking."

As soon as his mother's back was turned, Tubby Bear started to throw flour around the kitchen. Everything turned white as though it was snowing.

Then he tried to juggle with three eggs, but they soon ended up on the floor.

SPLAT!

"Scrambled eggs!" laughed Tubby.

Next he put the
mixing bowl on his
head and pretended
it was a helmet.

"Tubby! I told you to wait for me," shouted his
mother when she saw what her son had done.

Tubby Bear jumped with fright and the mixing
bowl spun off his head and on to the floor.

CRASH!

"My best mixing bowl!" sobbed Mrs Tubby.
"You bad bear, you can't help me with the baking
now. Go out into the garden. And don't disturb
your father."

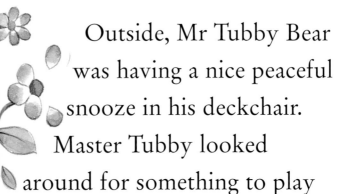

Outside, Mr Tubby Bear was having a nice peaceful snooze in his deckchair. Master Tubby looked around for something to play with, and saw his ball. First he kicked it into the middle of his father's favourite flowers.

Then he kicked it against Mr Tubby's deckchair, and woke him up.

And then he kicked his ball hard and high.

CRASH!

It broke the bathroom window.

"Tubby Bear!" growled his father. "You did that on purpose, didn't you? I think you had better go to your room until you learn how to be good."

"What about the tea party?" asked Tubby, who was beginning to feel sorry for being so naughty.

"We'll just have to see if you are obedient enough to join in," replied his father.

All afternoon, Tubby Bear was as quiet as a mouse. He didn't want to miss the fun of the tea party. He read his book. He drew a picture for Mrs Tubby Bear. He even tidied his room.

At four o'clock Noddy and Big-Ears arrived for tea. It was very quiet at Tubby Bear's house.

"Where's Master Tubby ?" asked Noddy.

Mr Tubby then explained.

"I expect he'll be hungry by now," laughed Big-Ears. "It's hard work being good."

"Yes," said Mrs Tubby, "I think I'll check on him."

"Now Tubby," said Mrs Tubby Bear, "if you promise to be good and helpful, you can come down for tea with Noddy and Big-Ears."

"Oh yes, I promise," said Tubby happily, and ran downstairs.

At the table Tubby was very polite. He handed round the plates and the sandwiches and the cake.

"Where has Tubby Bear gone?" asked Noddy. "You are not the same naughty bear who threw a ball at me this morning!"

Tubby Bear laughed.

"Would you like some milk in your tea?" he asked.
He reached across the table for the milk jug and...
oh no! It fell on to the floor with a

CRASH!

Tubby Bear began to cry. He had tried so hard to
be good.

"Never mind," said Mrs Tubby. "It was an
accident, and we all have those."

"Yes, and we really are having a smashing tea party," said Big-Ears.

"Especially Master Tubby!" said Noddy, and everyone laughed.

THE NODDY CLASSIC LIBRARY
by Enid Blyton™

Available in hardback
Published by HarperCollins